COMMANDER TUCKAHARMIN

(VOLUME 3):

FINDING TED

Jacob Brancu Greene
&
Aanand Yu

OTHER BOOKS BY COCO-A-LO PRODUCTIONS:

Skeleton No-Name & That Guy Who Never Showed His Face (Until Now!)

Commander Tuckaharmin Vol. 2:
The Unveiling of Skeletora McWig

Princess Engineera vs. The Money Snatcher

VISIT US AT:

http://www.blurb.com/user/store/mbrancu

http://mbrancu.wixsite.com/cocoaloproductions

This book was written by two kids, Jacob and Aanand. Jacob is 10 and Aanand is 11. They are neighbors and have been friends since Jacob moved to the neighborhood at the spunky age of 1. They are excited to share their love of epic LEGO space battles and earn money for A Lotta Love and Inter-Faith Council of Social Service in Carrboro, NC. The programs create a welcoming home environment for homeless women and children in the community.

Thank you for purchasing this book. 100% of the profits will be donated to these programs.

Acknowledgements: We would like to to thank Ms. Kathryn Cobb, Ms. Kim Mellor, and Ms. Delia Hudson for inspiring Jacob to improve his communication through speech and writing and to "put forth more effort!!"; Ms. Katherine Nicholson, Ms. Jennifer Litts Faul, and Ms. Laura Sorrese Lefkow for their review and feedback on this book; Small Hands Big Hearts United for supporting their efforts to raise funds for this important cause; and to our parents for helping us make this book happen.

Chapter 1:

The Capture

While Commander Tuckaharmin was fighting bad guys, he was wondering how his dad was doing. [Insert dramatic flashback to his dad's past life here... Okay, you got the picture? Let's move on.]

His father, Ted Tuckaharmin, retired from Skelecratic Uncivil Service 25 seconds ago. He used to be the lawyer to Ronald the Skeleton, the most famous gravedigger ever. He retired after lying in a sauna thinking about how annoying Ronald the Skeleton was. Ronald couldn't stand looking at human skin, and so therefore, he was annoying. Ted Tuckaharmin had human skin and Ronald the Skeleton kept yelling at his lawyer to hide it.

Skeleton No-Name, Commander Tuckaharmin's mortal enemy, had been trapped in space for 10 years. After he was rescued by a taco fanatic in a hover wheelchair, he decided to retire and have a simple life working as a gas station manager, spending his monthly paycheck on bacon. He never expected to come back out of retirement until ...

Pum-Pum-PUUUMMMMMMMMMM.......

One day, a man came in to fill up his ship's tank, and they got into a conversation. They talked about their deepest secrets.

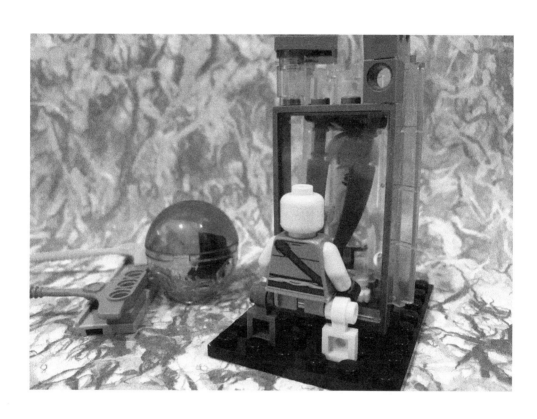

Skeleton No-Name noticed that the man was missing a hand and asked how he lost it. Ted Tuckaharmin said, "it runs in the family." He then forgot to pay and left. Skeleton No-Name felt some rage and then put 22 and 51 together and realized the connection. He had just been duped again by a member of the Tuckaharmin family.

He took his hover scooter to chase him.....

.... realized it was inefficient and breaking his back....
and dragged out his old spaceship.

He caught up to Ted, and pulled Ted's space motorcycle
with his ship's silver claws.

He then took him to Darkton.

He chose Darkton because it's dark and it's evil. As he was dragging Ted, he was laughing so hard that he almost crashed into a giant intergalactic slushy truck.

Chapter 2:

Darkton

Skeleton No-Name took Ted Tuckaharmin to Darkton because he knew Commander Tuckaharmin would search for him. He wanted to get revenge because Commander Tuckaharmin ejected him into space when he was super close to destroying him, and he had to deal with his annoying Evil Servant for 10 years.

Meanwhile... After Commander Tuckaharmin finished fighting bad guys for the day, he went to Tuckaharmin Hill for the usual Taco Thursday Daddy-Son Taco Time. His dad was nowhere to be found. He walked over to the gas station next door and asked the old gas station attendant if he'd seen him. (He didn't recognize Skeleton No-Name).

The attendant said, "Oh yeah (snicker snicker), he's over at (snicker snicker) Darkton (snicker snicker)." "What's so funny?" asked Commander Tuckaharmin. "I just ate some Snickers," said Skeleton No-Name. Commander Tuckaharmin walked away shaking his head thinking the old guy was a little banana-pie-in-the-head.

He got in his ship and set off for Darkton.

He unexpectedly hit a lot of space traffic. Let's just say that Commander Tuckaharmin had a very deep and old rage against space traffic. But that's a story for another time. Eh, whatever, I'll tell you now: When he was a young child, he and his dad got stuck in a lot of space traffic. His dad started honking the horn so hard that the safety airbag went "Poomph!" and hit dad in the face so hard that he had to go to the hospital. Ted Tuckaharmin barely made it. Tuckaharmins have very weak foreheads. And so Commander Tuckaharmin hated space traffic since then.

But then again, back to our story....

He forgot that today was the huge **F**ederal **A**wesome P**r**etty

Terrorists (FART) fashion show. FART is *THE* best terrorist

fashion show in the multi-verse.

Last year's most fashionable look was a fedora, a brown
trench coat with radioactive weapons hidden inside the
underwear, and a giant machine gun hidden in the back.
Every Evil-Doer was going to be there.

Chapter 3:

The Ultimate Trial, Part I

Commander Tuckaharmin entered Darkton, a giant black cube floating in space. After he landed, he went to the FART Stadium to see how horrible the fashion ideas were after last year. (Last year, he had given them a 1-star review on BadChat, social media news for Evil-Doers.)

This time, he got captured by guard police, evil police that protect Darkton from Do-Gooders.

If you ask Commander Tuckaharmin, he'd say that they *SHOULD* be protecting space from themselves. But, then again, nobody asked Commander Tuckaharmin.

Commander Tuckaharmin is known throughout the galaxy as the Ultimate Do-Gooder. He received his badge from Ronald the Skeleton, who gave it to him for saving his pet Space-Rat, "Senior Bobo The Twenty-Seventh and a Half". He also earned 52 other Trophies of Awesomeness.

He got sent to Do-Gooderville, a prison camp. It had 13 Good people, who had also gotten captured elsewhere, all trying to escape by painting themselves orange and declaring themselves "Neutral" to be released. The guards don't care about Neutrals, ordinary citizens who don't take sides. The guards' motto is "Neutrals are orange to us." So, they painted themselves orange.

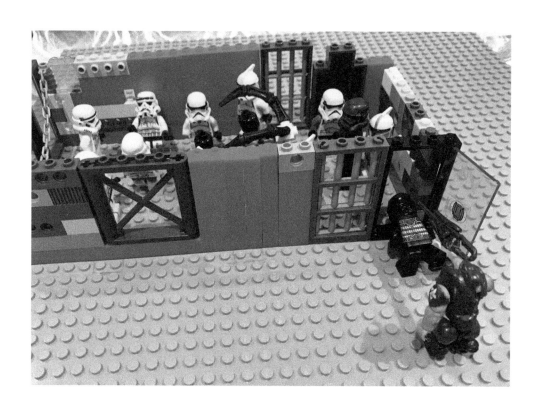

Commander Tuckaharmin decided to go the old fashioned way by crawling under the fence. Unfortunately, he got captured again. So he decided to befriend the 13 people and go with the "Neutral" plan.

The 13 people were all orange, but upon further inspection, he realized that they were actually the 13 droids that Skeletora McWig used to help capture him in the last book. They turned to Good once Commander Tuckaharmin introduced them to the amazing Broccoli Tacos.

[Hey, you! Yeah, you. The one reading this book. Just in case you're confused, the 13 Good people and the 13 droids are the same.]

The guards came over to make sure that the Good people were actually orange and declared that they were not Neutral. At first the droids did not know why. But then they realized that their paint was too dark of a shade of orange – it looked too much like red.

Since their orange scheme did not work out, they decided to make use of the things that they had previously stolen from the prison kitchen.

They had: butcher knives, rice, water, seaweed, avocado, and a touch of soy sauce. They also had some random pieces of iron, an old gigantic soda bottle, and a little thing that spins around when you push a button on it. And so, Commander Tuckaharmin pulled an "Iron Chef" and created the Shark-shi: A Shark sushi machine gun with a shark double-barrel blaster that shoots sharks. They created a killer sushi: Seriously tasty. Seriously deadly.

When the guards walked by, a sushi with a shark head pounced from the building and gobbled one of them up. The other ran away.

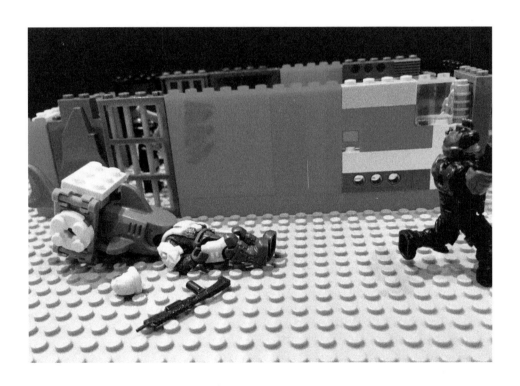

Chapter 4:

The Ultimate Trial, Part II

Afterwards, they used their Shark-shi to blast through the fence, get away, and figure out what to do next. The droids placed themselves around the perimeter of the prison to keep a lookout in case any meddling guards came by.

The emergency perimeter alert was a whistle. Commander Tuckaharmin saw a sign that said "Tuckaharmin Family Zoo This Way." Clearly the Tuckarmin family was *NOT* well liked on Darkton. [insert devil emoji here].

He followed the sign and found a giant prison. The shape of the prison looked a lot like Skeleton No-Name's head with barbed wire on top and had been paid for by FART.

Commander Tuckaharmin disguised himself as a moving upside-down cabinet. As he "sneakily" scraped the cabinet across the floor, he noticed there were bones on display behind glass cases and hidden white lasers in the back of the prison cells. The bones behind the glass cases were from past Tuckaharmin family members. He recognized his grandfather's spaceball cap in one of them.

Just then, a guard saw the cabinet moving, and saw a piece of black-and-red cloth peeking out from one of the drawers. He sent the signal to the other guards. Then one by one the guards came rushing toward the prison.

The droids, who were keeping a lookout, tried to whistle. Unfortunately droids do not whistle. Instead, they made static-like beeps – a whistle in droid language. Commander Tuckaharmin didn't recognize the sound and thought they were just communicating with each other. So he got caught.

As he was getting carried away, he passed by a cell and saw his father snoring inside.

He got placed in the cell right across from Ted.

The droids realized the beeps were an ineffective signal when Commander Tuckaharmin did not come running out 5 minutes later. They ran around trying to find a random Neutral to whistle for them. But they didn't find any because the Neutrals were all at the FART Stadium. So the droids rushed in along with a Shark-shi friend.

One of the security guards who had previously encountered the Shark-shi, which had devoured his friend, said, "Oh no! Not another one!" and ushered the rest of the guards out.

Then fainted from fear.

Let's pause here for a moment and go back in history a bit. Way back when Commander Tuckaharmin was still in baby diapers, Skeletora McWig had shorter hair and went to Neutral school with Senior Taco the Third. They were friends. When school ended, they went their separate ways. Skeletora McWig went into the family business of pestering Tuckaharmins. Senior Taco the Third went on to be a Neutral. He took on the family business of running the Taco Theme Park and making sure the free samples of tacos were fully stocked. Senior Taco the Third had to keep the business running, so he started making droids (all the rage in that day – a bit like feather earrings in 1987) to sell in the stock market to make money for his park.

One day, Skeletora McWig was shopping for eggplants at the local bazaar. She saw Senior Taco the Third and struck up a conversation with him. When she heard that he needed money to keep his theme park going, she felt a small amount of pity for him and bought his 15 droids that he was selling there. She also thought that perhaps they might be useful to her. Two droids would be used as mannequins for her wigs, the other 13 would be for pestering. If you're confused about the wigs, go back and read the second book. It will explain everything. What?! You haven't read that one? What are you doing reading this one, then?? Okay, go out, buy the first book and the second book, read them all the way through and then come back and finish this one.

After you've read those books, we might as well jump to 15 years in the future... in the past. Senior Taco the Third was testing out the Taco Chariot, his new Taco Roller coaster at his theme park. While he was riding, the taco shell part of the seat cracked off and he fell and broke his legs. Since then, he's needed to use a blue hover wheelchair to get around.

Now that you know the history, we can go back to what's happening right now...

Senior Taco the Third was spending his monthly paycheck on quesadillas when he heard the beeping sound from one of his favorite droids, Joe Billy Bob. He hovered over to investigate. He found 13 droids. He noticed their ID tags with his logo on them and remembered they were his 13 droids that he made for an old friend, Skeletora McWig. They told him what happened in beeps and crackles. He only understood it because he activated the translator on his control board underneath his chin. He decided to help the droids do their task because they were his babies.

He was able to sneak into the prison because the guards didn't care about Neutrals. He saw a big button right next to the entrance that said, "Turn off all lasers." As a Neutral who was also a ninja (a "Neutrinja"), he did a very unnecessary back-flip with his hover wheelchair and smacked the button with his feet, unlocking all the cells. That ninja move pressed his legs into their sockets, which hurt a lot, so he screamed in pain. The guards heard the noise, went toward the scream, and didn't notice all the prisoners escaping.

Ted was still snoring. Commander Tuckaharmin dragged his dad out of the cell. Ted woke up and said, "What did I miss? Where's the food? Are you here to deliver the flip-flops I ordered? And where is everybody?"

The guards looked at Senior Taco the Third and said, "Oh, it's just a Neutral who broke his legs. Nobody cares, let's go." They went back to their posts and noticed that all the prisoners, including the Tuckaharmins, were no longer there.

The white lasers were no longer active.

They froze in fear.

Once thawed out, they said, "My job is over." And they raided the paycheck safe and ran away to hide in the deepest pits of Darkton.

Chapter 5:

The Revelation

Meanwhile, the Tuckaharmins fled to Commander Tuckaharmin's ship and flew off to Planet Unpronounceable, fighting against the hated space traffic. Commander Tuckaharmin was smacking the horn so hard that his hand went right through the steering wheel. Once the horn was broken, they resolved instead to make loud farting noises through the air vents for all to hear.

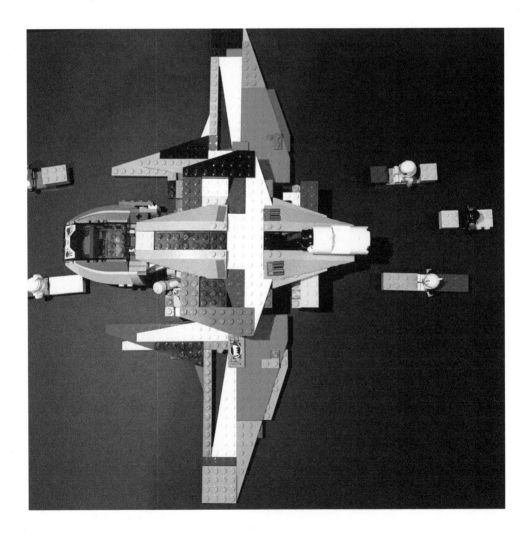

In just 48 hours, they made it back home. They had their annual Daddy-Son taco time. Usually they have it on a Friday. But today? It's on a ... Friday.

Now relaxed, the Tuckaharmins strolled over to the gas station to get back at Skeleton No-Name. Unfortunately he was gone.

Skeleton No-Name was on his lunch break…. at Senior Taco the Third's Taco Theme Park on Darkton awaiting the FART Fashion Show. He was also there to check on his new Tuckaharmin Family Zoo. When he actually got around to checking on it, he suddenly and dramatically realized why he wasn't immediately rich from this zoo. The Tuckharmins were gone. He said, "Holy Macaroni Bananas and Pie With a Bit of Smoke on The Side!" And then he fainted. (How do skeletons faint anyway? They don't even have any nerves!)

Back on Planet Unpronounceable at the gas station, Commander Tuckaharmin was looking at some magazines titled, "Mom." They were about moms. He started thinking about moms and realized that he never interacted with his own.

He asked his dad about where his mom was.

"Son," Ted said, "I adopted you."

Commander Tuckaharmin flailed his arms and said, "If I was adopted then where are my real parents? And why is my hand cut off like yours?" Ted replied, "Because I cut it off. It's a family tradition."

He explained that Commander Tuckaharmin's real father, Bon Bon Boy, and mother, Oogeley Boogeley, are the most notorious villains in the known universe. Once, they stole all the pizzas in the universe!

[How HORRIFYING is THAT??!! For a year, nobody could survive without that tasty cheese and sauce].

Now that he knew about his past, Commander Tuckaharmin felt bad that his real parents missed out on having a Do-Gooder life.

He vowed to find them and turn them into Do-Gooders.

Find out how... in Book Four!

Thank you for your donation to a great cause!

For more information about our mission and our partners:

Inter-faith Council for Social Service:
http://www.ifcweb.org

A Lotta Love:
http://www.alottalove.org

Small Hands Big Hearts United:
http://www.smallhandsbigheartsunited.com

About CoCo-A-Lo Productions

Jacob and Avery are 10 and 7 years old. When Jacob was 8, he hated writing in school. His mother encouraged him to write about his greatest love. So naturally, he chose to write about epic Lego space battles. Then he self-published the book, donating the profits to the Donate-A-Room program (now called A Lotta Love) of the Inter-Faith Council of Social Service in Carrboro, NC. The program creates a welcoming home environment at a homeless shelter for women and children.

This inspired his sister, who decided to write her own book and support this cause. And they inspired several next-door neighbors, Tristan (11), Olivia (9), and Aanand (11), who co-authored additional books and helped with fundraising for the shelter.

Jacob and Avery's goals are: "to raise $700, write 10 books, give a home to at least one homeless family, and inspire 5 other kids." Thank you for helping them reach their goal and helping a homeless family in need.

Keep up to date on their progress online at their website: http://mbrancu.wixsite.com/cocoaloproductions

Lightning Source UK Ltd.
Milton Keynes UK
UKHW050815270519
343376UK00008B/303/P